Flash Meets the Orchestra

By Charlie Alexander

ISBN: Softcover   978-1-5245-1183-8
       Hardcover   978-1-5245-1184-5
       EBook   978-1-5245-1182-1

Print information available on the last page

Rev. date: 06/21/2016

To order additional copies of this book, contact:
Xlibris
1-888-795-4274
www.Xlibris.com
Orders@Xlibris.com

Flash Meets the Orchestra

Written by Charlie Alexander
Art work by Charlie Alexander

This book is intended to help children of any age experience the pallet of musical instruments and how they work together.

Thanks to my wife, Becky, for her love and encouragement.
And a hats off to my pal, Flash!

Flash was awakened by the alarm!

It was time to get up.
And start a big
adventure!

Flash was so excited!

He couldn't wait to go with Charlie.

So off went Flash and Charlie.

A ride in the car is always fun for Flash.

Charlie and Flash arrive at the Concert Hall

It was a very big building with a large concert hall.

The first instrument Flash heard was a Violin.

Violin

"How beautiful a sound!" thought Flash.

And then Flash thought he saw another Violin.

Viola

But Flash was surprised to learn that it was called a Viola.
He thought it sounded just a bit lower than the Violin.

Do you know which one is a little bigger?

Violin

Viola

They do look very much alike!

There's always room for Cellos

"Cellos are bigger still and have a deeper sound."
thought Flash!

And then Flash saw a DoubleBass

"My goodness!" thought Flash." "It's twice as big as a cello and sounds so deep and low!"

Now both Flash and Charlie hoped to hear the Violins, Violas, Cellos and DoubleBasses all make such incredible sounds together.

"Surely this must be the whole orchestra!" Flash thought. He didn't know how many more instruments he would still be meeting before lunch time.

Violins, Violas, Cellos and DoubleBasses made up the String Section.

Flash had never heard anything like it before!

Flash didn't know that there were lots more surprises ahead.

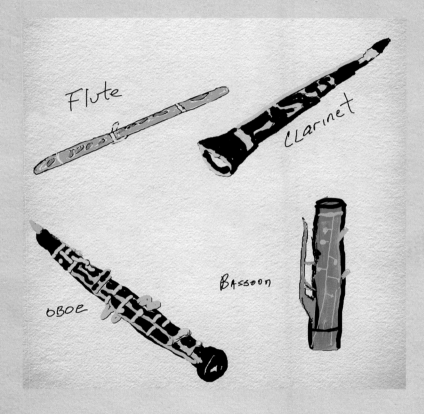

He had never heard the sound of a flute. He had never heard of an Oboe or Bassoon before. And he'd never seen a clarinet!

Flutes look like:

Flute

And sound like a gentle hollow breeze.

Oboes use a reed and look like:

Oboe

And sound like a duckling singing an exquisite melody.

Clarinets look a lot like an oboe, but have a much different sound.

Clarinets sound like smooth swirls of black licorice.

Bassoons sound a little like a friend of an Oboe.

But maybe like an older and bigger friend.

Flash thought, "How can there be so many wonderful sounds?"
The Woodwinds would join in with the String Section.

He smiled at the magical tones that filled the air.
Flash and Charlie were having the best day ever!

And now a nine and a half foot Piano was being rolled into place.

Flash was becoming anxious to see who was going to play
this huge black contraption, fully aware
that this was Charlie's favorite instrument.

"Wow! What a strong clear sound!" barked Flash.

This instrument is called a Trumpet.

Flash liked the French Horn best of all.

French Horn

Charlie knew it was because Flash is a "French Poodle".
These shiny new instruments are
called the Brass Section.

The Trombone had a slide arm that got longer or shorter for some notes.

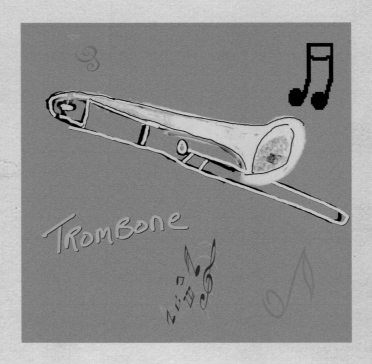

"TROMBONES ARE COOL"
was the look in Flash's eye.

The Tuba was the biggest
of the Brass Section

It also played the lowest.

Flash thought it was funny to learn that there are French Horns and English horns too!

Trumpets and Trombones, Tubas and something called a Euphonium were now making their entrance.

The Cymbals, the Triangle and the Timpani Drums along with the Piano are all part of the Percussion Section of the Orchestra.

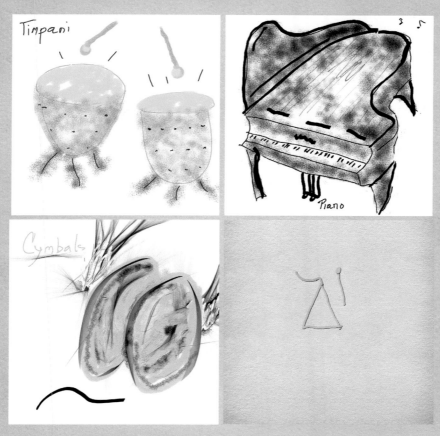

Instruments that are struck are part of the Percussion Section.

Cymbals, a Triangle and two great big
Kettle Drums were making an entrance.

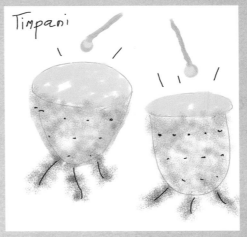

Flash could only wonder who would be in charge and who
would tell which instrument to play what and when!

Now Flash saw the Conductor of the Orchestra

The conductor seemed to be the one in charge.

The Conductor glanced at Charlie. He and the Orchestra were now ready to play Charlie's new composition!

In walked Becky, (Charlie's wonderful wife) and Flash knew it was finally time to hear the Orchestra play the Music Charlie had written. The best part was that Charlie was going to play the Piano part himself!

What a day! Flash will remember this day for a very very long time!

The End.

Printed in the United States
By Bookmasters